Great Aι

A wicke

E C Hι

 FABLE
NOOK

www.fablenook.com

Cover artwork: Amy Nolan

Contents

1 Arrival

Saturday – that's yesterday – my brother Alex was first to sound the alarm. 'Graham – Emergency!'

My kid sister, Jess, has been learning how to dial 999 at school, and she'd already got to 99 before Mum stopped her. 'It's alright sweetie, no need to panic. It's only your Great Aunt Bertha. She's come to stay a while.'

I've been studying the Second World War in history. The sound of those air raid sirens didn't leave my brain for the rest of that afternoon.

Great Aunt Bertha used to live in the northern most tip of Scotland. You can go no further without catching a boat to the Orkneys. What possessed her to move all the way south to Sussex is a mystery. Seems a few years ago she'd stayed down here a while, to sort out some business of her husband's. We reckon it was some life insurance scam. Afterwards, she went back to her northern wilderness. A dark castle no doubt.

Well, now she's back.

There we were, a happy family, in a state of near domestic bliss – the next thing – bang.

Alex had pulled me to the window to watch her arguing with the taxi driver. Poor bloke couldn't get her bags out the boot quick enough. 'Seventeen pounds?'

she shrieked. 'You must be joking. Fifteen and no more. And no tip. Be off with you.' And all this said in the strongest, upper crust English accent. Not that Great Aunt Bertha is English. In fact, no one really knows where she came from, or why we call her Aunt at all – some secret that Mum and Dad won't let us in on. Alex reckons she's Swedish. I think, more likely Martian...

Our house is not that big. Three bedrooms. That's one for me and Alex, one for Jess, and one for my parents. So, Great Aunt Bertha? Well, it's not that I don't like my sister, but last night, Great Aunt Bertha moved into Jess' room, so Jess moved in with us. Airbed on the floor. A small airbed because Jess is small. It's the rest that's taken up the space. Dolls, cots, Peter Rabbit books, Peter Rabbit himself – one ear missing, trapped in the car door when Jess was three – the lot.

Now it's midnight on the second day. Second day of hell – *Your trousers, Graham. Doesn't your mother iron them? Eat your cabbage. In my day, it was swede. Makes you big and strong. You're like a drooping dandelion –* And all that was before she'd pinched Jess' cheek and made her cry and informed Alex that his spotty face was the worst she'd ever seen.

It's dark, but I can make out a heap on the floor that is Jess, moving about. Now she's facing me, her eyes open. I close mine quick, but not quick enough.

'Graham, I can't sleep. Bed's too hard.'

Jess has one of those voices that demands attention. Thin, nasally, and being only seven years old, most insistent. The old airbed's sprung a leak, so I allow her to climb under my nice warm duvet.

School in eight hours. Up at 7.30. That's the latest I can make it to breakfast and still catch the bus. Aunt Bertha's snoring cannot be ignored. I push my feet out the bed and press them to the carpet. Jess moves to the wall, gripping Peter Rabbit hard to her chest, pulling the covers over her – all of them.

Jess' room, now Aunt Bertha's, is two steps along the landing. The door is open. Great Aunt Bertha is lying on her back; her mountainous head of hair is barely covered by a huge hairnet. She's rather skinny, with a pointed nose – and has the snores of a walrus. I pull the door to. It creaks. Great Aunt Bertha is up like a shot.

'Who's there?'

'Just me, Great Aunt Bertha. I couldn't sleep.'

'Nonsense. Of course you can sleep. You just need to try harder. Where's my handbag. Left it on the side last night. What have you done with it?'

'Me?'

'Wake your parents. We shall see about this. You're after money for your fix no doubt. You youngsters are all the same. Annabel! Annabel!'

There's muttering from behind my parents' bedroom door. Mum arrives in her pyjamas.

'What's going on Graham?'

'Great Aunt Bertha says I've taken her handbag.'

Great Aunt Bertha is edging towards me, bony finger outstretched. All six foot of her. The hem of her nightdress flops around her ankles, except the back of it, which has somehow got tucked into her bloomers, revealing her left leg, which is as skinny as a coat hanger, and her bulbous knee.

'He's got my handbag!' Her voice is shrill, like Jess, only ten times as loud.

I see her handbag on the floor next to the bed. It's exceedingly large. Leather I'd guess. I point to it and look at Mum. She shoos me back to my bedroom and I go, willingly. Back under the covers, I lie awake, listening to Mum's hushed tones and Great Aunt Bertha's loud ones. It's difficult to make out exact words in the mush of it all, except for the occasional, *handbag* and *drugs*.

Having something to listen to is oddly soothing.

A hand drops onto my face. Jess is asleep. Peter Rabbit seems to have lost favour in preference to Beatrix, her favourite doll, who in turn has lost most of her hair. An idea comes to me. It concerns revenge – and Aunt Bertha's hair. An idea that includes flour, and a hairnet. I drift off to sleep thinking about the wickedness of it.

2 Enough is enough

I awake to two empty beds. Jess' flat airbed and Alex's heap. Forgetting Jess is beside me, I roll over and cause a scream. It's not Jess that I've squashed – it's Peter Rabbit. Jess explains in a high-pitched squeal that Peter has had tummy ache all night long, and now I've squashed his belly.

The reason for my waking at all is Mum's voice. A different sort of scream. 'Graham-Graham, you'll be late again!'

She's right about the *again*. Three times last week. I jump out of bed, apologise to Peter Rabbit, and dress quickly; forgetting Jess is there, staring at me, like she's taking notes.

I hurtle down the stairs, three at a time. Alex is at the table, smartly dressed; neat tie, trousers pressed. You could cut your hand on the crease. Brothers, but you'd never think it. My fair hair, his dark hair – my blue eyes, his brown. Not the only difference. He's a real swot. Would've made it to grammar school if there was one. Me? Happy enough where we both ended up: St Luke's Comprehensive. Mixed. Suits me. Better scenery.

'Cornflakes?' Mum is already pouring them into a bowl. Jess arrives, still in her pyjamas. Peter Rabbit, it seems is having a well-earned rest in my bed. It's Beatrix she's feeding, clutching the plastic doll in her lap, offering the little pouting mouth real cornflakes and real milk, all of which dribbles to Jess' lap. Maybe Mum will stick the whole of her straight in the bath before school.

I guess Great Aunt Bertha might also be having a lie-in, like Peter Rabbit. I am wrong. The back door rattles and swings open as if a great wind has struck it – its handle smashing into the plaster.

And there she is, like a giant – pink floppy tracksuit covering those skinny legs.

'Good run?' Mum asks.

'Five miles,' Great Aunt Bertha puffs. She puffs so hard, I can see her false teeth blowing in and out of her mouth, only prevented from shooting me, by those thin pale lips. 'Up since dawn. Not like you, Graham. Early to bed, early to rise...'

She has pink sneakers on her large feet, and her hair is tightly enclosed under a huge blue bathing hat. I've not seen many bathing hats, and never one like this. The rubber strap under her chin is preventing the whole contraption from exploding under the pressure of that concealed hair. She blunders past me, and bangs the back of my chair. The spoon in my cornflake bowl launches itself and splatters us both in soggy orange flakes.

'Stupid boy!'

I say nothing. By not responding, I am being more than polite – and tolerant.

Mum glares at me. 'Say sorry, Graham.'

What? Me say sorry? Great Aunt Bertha is standing there. She too is glaring at me. Jess is glaring at me. The bald Beatrix is glaring at me. Alex picks up his school bag and heads for the open door.

'I am sorry, Aunt Bertha.'

Her glare slips sideways to meet Jess' eyes – Jess, who has started to giggle. With two short strides, the woman is upon her. Beatrix is removed from Jess' outstretched fingers and tossed into the sink. Jess is welling up. I guess only terror prevents an all-out scream.

'Aunt Bertha, please!' Mum says, over-politely.

I cannot understand the power this woman has. But anyone who does that to my sister… My thoughts return immediately to my wicked idea, not so wicked after all for someone who deserves it.

This is war.

3 First revenge

Night. I am restless: something on my mind. It's Aunt Bertha, squirming, because…because… Exactly, because of what?

Then I get to thinking. Who's the problem here; is it me, somehow misunderstanding the woman? But no, facts are facts: she made the first move, made my little sister cry. How would I feel, being seven years old and seeing my favourite cuddles thrown in the sink by a witch? She must be taught a lesson.

At what point I drop off, I cannot tell. I suppose no one can – but upon waking, it hits me: not hair, not yet, but tracksuit and sneakers. Nothing too serious. Just annoying. I check my phone. Not even six. I still have time, and am out the bed like a shot, and, stepping over Jess – whose airbed has been repaired by Alex – tiptoe downstairs to the back door. The witch's sneakers must be here…but no.

I hear the bathroom door open – and shut. Must be her. No one else gets up this early.

I'm up the stairs like a rocket and misjudge my landing. Crashing as noiselessly as possible, I silently scream as my knee hits the top step. But I am up. Her door is open, revealing her sneakers by the bed, shining bright pink under the glare of the bedside lamp.

I am quick. If she catches me I'm toast. One lace is undone and it pulls easily from the shoe.

I hear the toilet flush. No time for anything else.

As I dive back into bed, Jess stretches. I pray she won't wake up, and cover my head, listening.

The bathroom door opens.

The bathroom door closes.

Aunt Bertha's bedroom door closes.

I wait.

Nothing. No commotion. No rant.

It's getting hot under the covers and I poke my head out to breathe.

A towering silhouette greets me – a great beast looming in the doorway. This shock is followed by a mixture of fear and annoyance as the monster rips the covers from my bed.

The light comes on.

Alex swears.

Jess screams as the witch ventures further into the room.

And still she says nothing. Her plain white nighty drags on the floor. Not a witch: a ghost. Her hair is crammed beneath what must be the strongest hairnet in the world.

But it is the hand that thrusts towards me that is most striking of all, for within it is a dripping toilet brush.

There are limits, and I have met mine.

I hand over the shoelace, and Aunt Bertha glides out of the room. I am convinced her feet never touch the floor.

Alex shrugs.

Jess gives me one of those disdainful looks that only a freckled seven-year-old can. As if she can't bear the disappointment in her own brother, she turns over and gives Peter Rabbit a big hug.

But I have another plan.

That afternoon, after school, Aunt Bertha returns from her run, and as usual, after getting changed, presents her pristine pink tracksuit to Mum for washing.

My chance. My new jeans. Inexpensive. In fact, cheap. Very cheap. Never been washed before. But I need an accomplice.

As the start button of the washing machine is pushed I raise my finger, and Jess, waiting in the hallway, screams. A very loud scream. 'Spider!'

I press, *Reload*, and within seconds my *so* very cheap jeans are having a one to one with Aunt Bertha's top quality tracksuit.

Job done. Almost. This time I will play the innocent. Not fair on Mum, but all in a good cause. Aunt Bertha needs to learn, it's not just me; she needs to know this is an unsafe household. Who knows what might happen next? Best she doesn't stick around.

I give the wash a good half-hour just to be sure...

'Mum? Have you seen my new jeans? I left them on the wash pile.'

The following morning, as Aunt Bertha returns from her run, I am not simply surprised, I am overwhelmed by her chirpiness.

She smiles, allowing her false teeth to flap about as she pants for breath. 'You know, Annabel, it's was so good of you to let me know about that little washing accident. But really, what do you think? Goes well with my shoes. Pink and grey-blue. Quite something!'

Score: Aunt Bertha, two. Me, zero.

Jess glares at me. It is a glare that says: *my brother is a failure.*

Tuesday evening and Jess is working on a plan of her own. I am not allowed in our bedroom. I have to endure Aunt Bertha's company as she watches a soap on TV with Mum. There are several terrible things happening all at once: a car wreck, boy and girlfriend break-up, and a chimney about to fall into the street if someone doesn't do something to stop it right now. I leave the room as a burly fireman arrives to save the day. Even English homework is better than this. I spend forty minutes in the kitchen, scribbling, and shove my homework back into my schoolbag hanging in the hallway.

Creeping up the stairs, so as not to disturb the soap-watchers, I knock on our bedroom door and Jess opens it.

'Secret,' she says.

I enquire no further – probably best that I don't know – and return to the sitting room. Mum smiles. Aunt Bertha doesn't. Her eyes are glued to the screen, as shortly are mine. Another soap, but this time with scantily clothed lifesavers on an Australian beach. I'm looking at the girls. Not sure about Aunt Bertha.

Wednesday morning, there is no silhouette. No silent arrival. Aunt Bertha storms in.

'Your doing, Graham. Unpick them now!'

'Unpick what?' I say in all innocence.

Jess is oddly quiet, almost certainly squeezing Peter Rabbit under her covers.

Alex sits up. 'Ugh?'

The light goes on, and I see the tracksuit trousers dangling before my eyes. The end of each leg is sewn closed. The sewing is not perfect, and presumably one reason why Aunt Bertha suspects me. I have to give it to Jess – good job.

With the arrival of Mum and Dad at the bedroom door, I admit my guilt and spend the next twenty minutes in the kitchen, undoing Jess' handiwork.

Aunt Bertha is late for her run that day, and we don't see her return before we leave for school.

Jess grins at me as I leave.

I grin back.

Dad has a flicker of a grin too.

Mum however, does not. 'Don't meddle, Graham. You don't know what she's been through. Enough. You've had your fun. Leave her be.'

I see Aunt Bertha in the street. There's no avoiding our meeting. She stops in front of me, her hot breath smothering my air.

'Think you can play jokes on me, Graham Hopkins, and get away with it?'

She storms off, like Jess throwing a tantrum.

4 Silver lining?

School.

English is the first subject of the day. Not my favourite. I can't see why I have to learn about past participles when I can already speak the language well enough. I've not done my homework for the past three weeks and have run out of excuses. Mr Grant, it seems, has run out of patience and has threatened detention next time I fail to produce what he requires, and I'm pleased I spent some time on it last night.

The threat of detention usually works for me. For some, it's a rite of passage to the elite sect of students who are anti-teacher, anti-work – anti-everything. I'm not one of those, but there are so many other more interesting things to do...

The lesson goes surprisingly well, in that I'm not asked any questions.

Mr Grant is a stickler for correctness. And that includes the very process of handing in homework. At the end of a lesson, he stands by the door to receive our offerings. Mine is two pages long. Two pages of—

What?

Each page of my best handwriting is overwritten in black felt-tip: *I HAITE INGLESH*.

Each page! He'll go mad. I can't hand it in. What story would make any sense…? *It's my aunt. I dyed her trousers. The evil bitch is getting her revenge.* Or… *My kid sister. Must have been playing. She can't spell, see.*

No good. The first, though definitely true, is unbelievable: evil bitch of an aunt getting revenge? And the second, well I'm not lying about my sis in that way…

'Well, Hopkins?' Mr Grant always uses surnames.

'I err, forgot it. Sir.'

'Didn't do it, you mean. Detention. Here. Three-thirty. Don't be late.'

I'm pushed along by goody-goody James Thorcroft. Even his name sounds Shakespearian. His homework is presented in a clear plastic envelope. His handwriting is so clear it looks like newsprint.

Two others join me in detention. Mr Grant believes in running his own show, unlike some other teachers who are happy enough to stick everyone together in the hall or one of the bigger classrooms: History, Maths, Religious studies – all together. Old-fashioned detention: more of a punishment than extra learning to help the wayward student. The victims do something menial, like writing lines – a sort of brain washing. *I must treat teachers with respect.* Or, *I will learn to listen so I can learn.* Some of the Anti-brigade deliberately up their game in teacher-annoyance by changing the sentence: *I must talk slowly 'cos teachers are dumb.* Or other, more personal variations. Some of those in the higher ranks are well on their way to being expelled, or so they keep bragging.

Mr Grant is not one for giving his students ridiculous lines. No. We copy. And we copy in silence from some textbook he decides is appropriate. If he can't read the result, we rewrite and rewrite until he can read it, all of it, word for word. 'No good rushing,' he reminds us, ten minutes into the session.

So, three of us. And the subject to be copied: *Tom Brown's Schooldays*. Not the whole book, thank God, but the first two pages of hopelessly small print.

The sentences are long, complex. Unlike like the skirt of the girl sitting at the desk in front of me over to the right. Dark hair. She looks to be concentrating hard, writing slowly. I look at my own scribbles and slow down.

After an hour of near silence – broken only by the sighing and puffing from the boy behind – Mr Grant says, 'Claire Lester. Let me see.'

The girl goes to the teacher's desk.

He looks at her hard, then at her work. He smiles. 'Well done. You can go.'

Claire comes back to her desk to collect her bag and returns my lustful glare with a cheeky smile.

'Hopkins!'

Why just my surname? Am I inferior to the girl?

I approach the teacher's desk to learn the truth. He reads my offering: the occasional crossing out; a misspelled word – corrected. He'd be happy, surely that I'm trying to learn – correcting my mistakes.

'Not good, Hopkins. You'd do well to follow that girl's lead. She can teach you a thing or two.'

So, inferior after all. I wonder if Mr Grant understands what he just said. I'd rather have Claire Lester teaching me any day.

'Not good at all,' he repeats, handing back my scrawl, 'but I have better things to do. You may go.'

The third of our little trio, Matthew. Skinny. Always looks malnourished. He's sweating. He looks at me with frightened eyes, and it occurs to me he's not wearing his glasses. Without them, he's blind as a bat. He's written, as far as I can make out, half a page.

'Paxton!'

Curious, and a bit worried for Matthew, I wait, fiddling with my bag. He passes me on the way to his gallows. I turn to see his executioner glaring at the paltry offering. I can delay no longer and head for the door with that frightened image of him in my brain, and Mr Grant's words: 'Is that the best you can do, boy?'

A coward. I must be. I hurry through the door, and my mind suddenly presents me with a wicked image: Mr Grant and Aunt Bertha in a wrestling ring, and me as the ref. I'm still considering who should win, when I see Claire, heading out the school gate. Some boys – and girls – are following her, giving wolf-whistles and shouting abuse. I recognise members of the Anti-brigade, and run to the other side of the road, before slowing to a fast walk. A good few cars and bikes race by; enough cover, I reckon, not to be recognised. Hopkins to the rescue.

I cross the road and catch up with her. 'Hello. Don't take any notice of them, they're just idiots,' I say brazenly.

'Oh, them,' she says. 'Losers.'

As we walk together, we discuss Claire's expertise in copying tiny print, and other such interesting topics, like whether ants know what they're doing, and she lets slip her address: Harbuth Street. The whistlers are well gone, and I say goodbye. My mind turns to other things – like Aunt Bertha.

5 Spying

Over the next couple of days, odd things happen to Aunt Bertha: the delicious doughnuts, mysteriously filled with toothpaste, and the worm in her bed. But most spectacular of all, the flour descending on her head on opening her bedroom door.

Needless to say, Mum and Dad are not too pleased with the way things are going. Neither am I. Aunt Bertha is still here, and now my science homework has disappeared. Another detention is unavoidable, and I meet Claire again, this time in the hall. We're friends now. At least on speaking terms. I give her some gum. She says thanks. I smile while I write for the hundredth time: *I will do my science homework.* Claire writes: *I will no longer wear short skirts.* I know this because she shows me her writing, and the lines half way down the page, with the, *no longer*, mysteriously missing.

The following day is uneventful. To add a little excitement, I hand in my science homework.

Suddenly it's Friday. I decide to go the long way home. Harbuth Street. Claire lives around here somewhere. Told off by the maths teacher yesterday. Another teacher saying her skirt's too short. Seems they're all female... Thing is I don't think it's really hers. She's got an older sister. A hand-me-down I reckon.

This is the road. Long row of terraces, slate roofs, front gardens mostly gone. No parking here. Not even for residents. Main road. Cars parked where the gardens used to be. Nice bit of green on the other side of the road, and a playground. Lots of mums, and their toddlers. Swings, seesaws. Even a climbing frame shaped like a helicopter and—

Hello, I recognise her...that woman. Can't be. Aunt Bertha? All togged up in her running gear. Sitting there, on the park bench, bold as brass, just watching. Right there. They must've seen her. You could hardly miss that odd coloured tracksuit and bright pink sneakers. I don't believe it. She's only got her phone out...taking pictures.

Here comes Claire.

'Watcha,' she says, still chewing. Can't be the same gum...

'You ok? No detention today then?'

'Didn't notice my skirt?'

I might be going red. I always notice her skirt, and her dark hair. Dark eyes too. 'No, I mean...'

She smiles. I start to melt.

'I found an old one. Holes in it. My sister was chucking it. I cut it up and sewed a strip on the hem of this one. Only a bit. Nearly to the knee. Like the flair?'

She gives a little twirl. I like it very much.

'What are you doing here? Not following me?'

'How can I be following you. I got here first.'

'But you know where I live.'

She's rumbled me. 'Just a different way home.' I want to change the subject, and actually have something else to say. 'You see that woman over there, in the park, by the swings?'

'Yes, with the pink sneakers?'

'That's the one. What do you think she's doing?'

Claire shrugs her shoulders. 'Watching. A gran maybe. You been reading spy books?'

'Not a gran. She's my aunt. Great Aunt Bertha. But not my real aunt. No relation. She's staying with us. From the north of Scotland.'

'Maybe they don't have many children up there. Maybe she just likes them.'

'That's what I was thinking. She likes them. A bit too much. You know what she did just now?'

Claire raised her eyebrows. Nicely shaped. 'I expect you're going to tell me.'

'She took a picture. Bold as anything.'

'So?'

'So, she's horrible. Shouts at us – mostly me. Made my little sister cry. Something wrong with her. And now I see her taking pictures of little boys and girls. You think that's innocent?'

'Don't know, Graham.'

I realise we've been standing in the same spot for near five minutes.

She throws me a glance. 'Got to go. That's where I live. See that red car. My mum's boyfriend. He's bad news. Thinks he owns the place. I'm worried about Mum. Maybe see you tomorrow?'

'Yes, ok. Bye.'

I watch as she walks away, just two doors down, her elongated skirt swinging from side to side. She turns to squeeze past the red car and gives a little wave, and is gone.

Someone else is gone too. Aunt Bertha. I scan the park and the road, and see in the distance, just beyond the number 42 bus, a pair of bright pink sneakers running away from me.

I get back home to find Aunt Bertha in the kitchen talking to Mum. '...chatting to some floozy with a short skirt,' she's saying.

I ignore her, say a quick hello to Mum and go upstairs. 'Homework,' I say. 'Need to catch up.'

Not much chance of that. Jess is in our shared bedroom, playing Supergirl with her Barbies.

She catches me off-guard, and a Barbie hand is rammed up my left nostril. 'Ouch!'

'Sorry, Graham. She didn't mean it. She's on a mission.'

'To do what?'

'Save the world, silly!'

And that's just what I need to do: save the world from our Great Aunt Bertha.

6 Stakeout

Being Saturday, I have a lie-in. I might go for a walk later, go past Claire's house. I look at my phone and think I should give her my number. Who knows, one day she might need some help, or maybe a chat…or something. Already gone ten. Jess is up. I can hear her downstairs, protesting about eating her boiled egg.

Alex looks to be asleep, half his duvet resting on the floor alongside some book with a picture of Shakespeare on its cover. Thanks to him, I handed in my science homework yesterday. Useful sometimes being a year behind. Didn't quite copy his old work. Put in a couple of mistakes to make it look real. Something about magnets repelling. Should get good marks.

'Alex? You asleep?'

'Yes,' comes the daft reply.

'You know Aunt Bertha?'

'No.' Another daft reply.

'I saw her yesterday.'

'Don't say?' Alex sits up and ruffles his hair. 'Who turned the light on?'

'The sun,' I say, somewhat impatiently. 'I mean I saw her doing something odd.'

'As always.'

'She was in the park; you know that one down Harbuth Street.'

Alex slides off his bed and rescues Shakespeare before sitting back against his pillows. He opens the book and starts to read.

'You're not listening, Alex. She was in the park, watching children. Little children.'

'So?' Alex closes his book and sighs, like he's resigned to some persistent irritation.

'So, it's not normal. She was taking photos.'

'You think she's some kind of weirdo?'

I hoik myself up on my elbow and make a big thing of staring at my brother. 'Well she is, isn't she? Anyone else, you might not think anything of it. But she *is* a weirdo.'

'Time?'

'Just after ten.'

Alex drops Shakespeare back to the floor. There's a touch of arrogance in his voice. 'Not now. When you saw her.'

'Near four. A bit after. On my way back from school.'

'No detention?'

'Handed my homework in. You know that.'

Alex smiles. One of those smug grins. He gets out of bed and starts to rummage around for his clothes; with Jess sleeping in the same room, there's no space for a chair to put them on. 'You know,' he says, 'she goes for her run the same time every day, on the dot. Ever noticed that? Half-seven in the morning. Don't know about afternoons, but she's usually back before five.'

This is it. I've got his attention; got him to listen.

Alex has found a sock. 'Maybe this afternoon, we can go for a walk. A walk in the park.' Another grin.

I think he's going to be a lawyer. All that clever speak. Name-dropping. He'll be quoting Shakespeare next.

'Ok. Deal,' I say. 'Now I'm hungry. Need food.'

That afternoon, while mum and dad are watching some afternoon film on telly, Alex and I make our escape. It's about a ten-minute walk to Harbuth Street. We arrive in plenty of time, but need to find somewhere to hide with a good view of the playground. There's nowhere on the street. Has to be the park. A few big trees dotted around. We guess Aunt Bertha will come up from the road so we stand behind the trunk of an oak, and peer back that way. I stare at the house where Claire lives, wondering if I might catch a glimpse, and find myself wondering what she wears when not at school. Jeans, maybe, if her sister's chucking any out...

'There,' Alex says.

We've been here not five minutes, and here comes Aunt Bertha. Quite a sprightly jogger for her age. Straight to the bench. But wait. It's occupied. Two women, chatting. She's not phased, is our Aunt Bertha. Plonks herself down at the end of the bench. Starts to chat as if she's known them all her life. A little girl runs up to one of the women. Aunt Bertha is holding out her hand and the girl gives her a high five, then runs off again, back to the helicopter climbing frame.

We watch for another good ten minutes. It's quite boring.

'Know what?' Alex says. 'If anyone is watching us, you know what they'll think?'

'Weirdos,' I say.

Alex goes to walk off. 'Seen enough. Harmless.'

Suddenly, Aunt Bertha is on the move. Not far. To a tree. Another oak as far as I can tell. Close to the swings. Starts doing those stretch things runners do, a pink sneaker raised to the trunk; pushing – keeping her other leg straight. She turns around, like she's going to do some other exercise, leaning against the tree, but then, with the speed of a jet fighter, raises her phone, and clicks.

'There,' I say, ecstatic. 'Told you.'

'Want to report her to the police?'

'No evidence. Unless...'

'Unless you can steal her phone, and her password of course.'

Alex should change his name to Sherlock.

'You saw her too,' I complain. 'Why me?'

Alex pulls me back out of sight. Talks low. 'Because you are the investigator. If it comes to it, I can be a witness. There's a way to go before we get to that stage.'

I don't say anything, but peer round the tree trunk – and come face to face with Aunt Bertha. She nearly crashes into me. Alex, as cool as anything, does a bunk, hightailing it to the safety of the other tree. I am alone with the witch. 'Aunt Bertha. What a surprise!'

'What are you doing here? Spying on me?'

'Spying? On you? No, of course not. I-I was just waiting that's all. You know for that girl...'

'Floozy.'

'Yes, that's right. No. No, she's not a floozy. She's nice. You'd like her...I think. She might even like you. I mean...'

'I know what you mean. Your mother shall hear about this. Your father too.'

She speeds off, first visiting the bench, waving to the two women. They wave back, and she heads for the road. A smooth operator is Aunt Bertha. I reckon she's part of the Orkney Secret Service. Just wait til they get my evidence.

Alex reappears.

'Coward,' I say.

We walk back to the road.

'So what's the plan?' Alex is grinning again. 'All that glitters is not gold.'

I knew it. I knew Shakespeare would get here sometime. 'And what is that supposed to mean?'

'What I say. Your precious evidence. Might look like the real thing, but there might just be another perfectly reasonable explanation.'

My mind is suddenly wrenched away from all thoughts of Aunt Bertha. A red car is pulling out of Claire's drive. It revs up with some big bore exhaust sounding like thunder, and zooms off. Standing in the doorway is a woman. She might be crying. Can't tell; too far away. A girl comes from behind her. A girl with dark hair, wearing jeans. She puts her arm around the woman and the door closes.

'Don't you think?' Alex is saying.

'What?'

'There's another explanation... Aunt Bertha.'

'Yes,' I reply, automatically. 'Probably. Expect so.'

I'm in a different world on the way home. A glimpse into Claire's life. Her private life. I had no right to see what I did, and even less right to remember it.

7 Search

Whether Aunt Bertha said anything or not to Mum and Dad, they haven't said anything to me.

I don't sleep too well, that image of Claire locked in my mind.

It might be Sunday, but none of us are church goers, except for Aunt Bertha. She has stated quite clearly that the English version of Christianity is a poor second to that practiced in the north of Scotland, where real people live and die by their wits alone. Still, an English church would have to do.

Having tossed and turned all night, I fall asleep as the sun rises and am rudely awakened by Aunt Bertha's bedroom door slamming. She is descending the stairs singing *Abide with me.* I shudder at the thought. The front door is next to slam. Not another noise for a full five minutes or more. An alarm clock is going off somewhere, and hurriedly silenced. Jess is sprawled out on her airbed. Alex is concealed somewhere beneath a pile of covers.

Once again awake, I can put my ridiculous dreamy thoughts of Claire to one side. I have work to do. A search of Aunt Bertha's room.

I tread carefully over Jess' killer Barbies, and creep out the door. Aunt Bertha's door is closed. Not surprising, considering the noise she made closing it.

Inside, the room is pristine. The bed is made with blankets and sheets. No flimsy duvet for one such as she. I make a note not to sit on it, a sure sign of some unholy transgression. Her phone, of course, is not there. My concentration will be better used finding something else, like...who knows what? I open the top drawer of the bedside cupboard. A single item: a Presbyterian Bible. I move on to the cupboard itself. Pink sneakers. Nothing more.

Someone is opening the bathroom door. I hear a cough and a grunt, and after another thirty seconds, the toilet flushes. The door opens, doesn't close. Must be Alex. Mum's always telling him off for leaving the bathroom door open. Maybe he'll see I'm not in bed. Maybe he'll guess where I am. I realise I'm standing rigid, my hand resting on the chest of drawers. I wait. Nothing.

I systematically try each of the four drawers. Clothes, so neatly folded. I check under each pile, memorising the exact position before disturbing anything; placing the pile back precisely as found. I'm in the bottom drawer. Underneath a pile of knickers is an envelope. Maybe she *is* Swedish, like Alex said. I'm not so sure. I mean, don't Martians wear knickers?

In the envelope are black and white photos. Must be years old. Boys and girls. Some in groups of twos and threes, but most, a good ten or more, of single boys and girls. On the back of many of them is some sort of code, as if relating to a catalogue: CB 17; CB 27, and so many more. I put them back. Exactly as I found them, except... two piles of knickers. Which one was it?

The front door slams. She's back. If she catches me, I'm toast. I shove the drawer closed and open the door. She's on the stairs. No time to get back to my bedroom. I pull the door closed and start down the stairs, pretending to yawn.

'Oh, good morning, Aunt Bertha.'

I back up to let the woman pass.

'Bible,' she says, brushing me to one side. 'Forgot it. First time in fifty-two years I forgot my bible. Must be this house. Must be you!'

She barges into her room and to my amazement sits on the immaculate bed and opens the top drawer of the bedside cupboard. I press my back against the wall as she sweeps past me and hurtles down the stairs.

She is gone, but the rest of the household is awake. My search is over. At least for today.

8 Truth

I get home on Monday afternoon at about four. No detention. And no Claire. Not at school as far as I could see.

Mum is in the kitchen. I guess Aunt Bertha has gone for her run, though I didn't see her at the park.

'Home early again,' Mum says.

'Yes. Been catching up with my homework, so no detention. Not sure about tomorrow though. English.'

Mum is filling the washing machine, cramming in a grey blanket. 'Give it a shove, Graham. Can't get used to Aunt Bertha's bedding. It'll take an age to dry.'

'Did it need a wash?'

'Who knows. Seems it's what she's always done. Monday is bed-change day. No getting round that.'

I fill the kettle and turn it on.

'Mum, do you think she's alright. In the head, I mean.'

Mum gives me one of those looks that tells me I'm about to get a telling off. It's those down turned corners of her mouth, and that barely perceptible squint.

'Your aunt has been through a lot in her life. A difficult childhood for a start. Then her husband of three weeks dying. I think she's entitled to be a bit odd.'

'I saw her in the park the other day, watching the children. She was taking pictures. We've had talks at school. They call it Safeguarding. All sorts of stuff about what some people get up to. They showed us newspaper articles, like where a man was done for keeping pictures of little children. And... and I found some pictures in her room, by accident I mean—'

The kettle makes that dinging sound when it boils and I reach for the coffee tin.

'I'm going to tell you something Graham, and you are to tell no one else, understand?'

I nod and start to make two cups of coffee.

Mum sits on the kitchen stool. 'There's all sorts of reasons why people take pictures. Not all bad. She's not your real aunt, you already know that. When your dad and me started out, we wanted to buy a house. Couldn't do it. No money for the deposit. I was up the park one day, sitting on a bench. It started raining. One of those showers you don't see coming. Except she did, this woman all dressed for winter. Had a brolly too. And there's me in my summer dress. I'd been shopping. Only thing I had was a paper bag. Didn't even cover my hair. Next thing, this woman sat next to me. Held her brolly over the both of us. A teacher. English teacher. Said I reminded her of someone. Someone she'd known long ago. I met her again, about a week later. We became friends.'

'But the pictures. They all have codes on them. CB, and a number.'

'Christian Brothers, Graham. Name of the—'

The back door swings wide open. Aunt Bertha is back from her run.

Mum looks at me. 'Not a word, Graham.'

Alex arrives too. Suddenly the kitchen is full. Aunt Bertha is asking about her blanket, Alex is checking the kettle and Jess is flying Barbies. Too much for me. I take my school bag upstairs, then go for a walk. Silly, but who knows I might bump into a certain someone near the park in Harbuth Street.

The park is not busy. Most of the mums have gone. I sit on a bench facing the road and stare across it to Claire's house. No red car. I'm glad, hopeful that the boyfriend is gone for good. But another car arrives. Parks right outside, on the road. Police car. No lights flashing. No big emergency. They get out. Both tall. Seem too tall for the little patrol car. The house door opens, but the policemen are in the way; I can't see who opened it. The door closes, and I feel alone, and a bit guilty too, for spying.

There's one mum, pushing her daughter on the swing. I find myself staring at them, at the swing moving back and forth, like a hypnotist's watch. I realise the woman is staring back at me, or should I say, glaring. I avert my eyes and go for a stroll around the field. When I come back, the woman and the little girl are gone – and so is the police car. Funny how I suddenly think of detention.

I should get back and do my English homework. One good thing about a brother who's a swot. Someone to look up too – and copy from.

I get back to a quiet house. Dad's not home from work. Alex is out and Mum's taking a break watching some soap on TV. But I can hear a woman's voice, and the occasional giggle. A little girl's giggle. I creep upstairs, and listen.

I recognise the story: Cinderella, and the part our Great Aunt Bertha is playing. She is the fairy godmother, just about to change Cinderella's tatty dress into a beautiful ball gown. A flood of emotions hit me. My little sister with this woman...my guilt at spying on Claire. If anyone, it's her that deserves a ball gown. Jess giggles again. It doesn't last for long. I fling the door open to see them both sitting on the bed, Aunt Bertha's arm around my little sister.

'What are you doing?' I yell. 'You leave my sister alone!'

Jess stares at me, horrified. But it is Aunt Bertha I'm really scared of. For just that instant as I'd opened the door, there'd been the last remnants of a smile. I'd never seen her smile before. All too late, I realise my error.

There's no hole in the world big enough to hide my shame.

'What do you think I'm doing?' Aunt Bertha screams. 'Get out. Out. Both of you!' She slams her door behind us and we are left on the landing staring at each other. Jess is trying to be brave, but her mouth is quivering, and her tears start to flow. I pick her up and cuddle her and go into our makeshift bedroom.

'I'm sorry Jess. I made a mistake. Got a few things on my mind.'

I'm expecting Mum to come through the door, but perhaps the slamming of doors and the odd scream is really not that unusual in our house.

I wipe Jess' tears with the end of my sheet, and she looks at me with those big eyes of hers and, as if so wise, starts to explain. 'You're silly, Graham. She was reading me a story. Cinderella. Got to the bit where Cindy gets a big dress. You spoiled it, Graham. She showed me her dolly. Calls it Lilly. Showed me a photo, black and white, of her baby. She had to leave it behind a long time ago. Her name was Lilly. They said she was too young to look after it. They gave it to someone else.'

My heart is thumping. My head is banging. Perhaps my brain is just a pot of some disgusting beef jelly. What have I done?

'She told me about her bed too. You know. All those blankets. She lived in a ophige.'

'Orphanage?'

'Yes that's it. What's a orphinge, Graham?'

'It's where children go if their parents are dead.'

Now I am feeling so bad, I almost want to rush back in there and give Aunt Bertha a big hug.

'That must be it.' Jess is not crying anymore.

'Did she tell you anything else?'

'Oh yes. Something about birds and bees, and a man at the orphinger. Says that's where Lilly came from. Said it was years ago. Says she can't forget. Makes her sad.'

There's a noise on the landing. A banging. And more bangs – on the stairs. Suitcases.

Jess is looking at me. 'Don't let her go, Graham. I like it when she reads to me.'

I wonder if there's a Shakespeare quote to fit my current situation, but I can find no words to express how I'm feeling. I just know Jess is right, and what I must do.

As we go down the stairs, I hear Mum.

'Aunt Bertha. You're leaving us?'

'That I am. And yee'll ne'er see me agin!'

Not Swedish. Not Martian. Scottish, through and through.

I can stand and watch – or do something. She's a strong woman is Aunt Bertha, but not as strong as a fit teenage boy. As I approach, a look of horror – and perhaps disgust – washes over her face. But she is slim, and my arms wrap around her easily. For the briefest of moments, I wonder when she last received a hug – and the last time I'd cried.

'Aunt Bertha. Don't go. I'm sorry.' I step back and am amazed to see her smile.

Jess is moving in for the kill, holding the woman's hand, looking up at her with those big brown eyes. 'Tell me about Cindy, Aunt Bertha. Did she get to the ball?'

Aunt Bertha crouches down and looks straight into Jess' eyes. 'I think I'd like a little cup of tea while Graham takes my cases upstairs; then we'll see.'

The following day, I meet Claire in detention, and afterwards we walk home and I tell her all about my Great Aunt Bertha, and how she's offered to help me with my English homework.

Claire tells me about her mum's boyfriend, and the drugs found in his car. But no, he's not coming back. As we get to her door, our hands meet, just for a second. She gives a little twirl, and a wave. 'See you tomorrow,' she says.

And I reply, simply, 'Yes. Tomorrow.'

That big hole? It's gone now. In its place is a mountain, and I'm on top of it.

All that glitters is not gold—

But some of it is...

Enjoyed this short story?
Go to www.fablenook.com to see what else is on offer.

Strange Doings at Nadgewicke

Beyond the void

Series - Helena Child of the Ancients:

Book One   Helena and the Secret of the Black Tower

Book Two   Helena and the Elixir of Life

Book Three   Helena and the Battle for Freedom

Printed in Great Britain
by Amazon